For Katherine
From Grandma and Pappy
Christmas 2008
With Much Love!

POLAR BEAR NIGHT

By Lauren Thompson • Pictures by Stephen Savage

SCHOLASTIC PRESS • • • • NEW YORK

10012. LIBRARY OF CONGRESS CATALOGING-IN-PUBLICATION DATA: Thompson, Lauren. · Polar bear night / by Lauren Thompson ; illustrated by Stephen Savage.—1st ed. · p. cm. · Summary: After wandering out at night to watch a magical star shower, a polar bear cub returns home to snuggle with her mother in their warm den. · ISBN 0-439-49524-5 (hardcover : alk. paper) · 1. Polar bear—Juvenile fiction. [1. Polar bear—Fiction. 2. Bears—Fiction. 3. Night—Fiction.] I. Savage, Stephen, 1965- ill. II. Title. · PZ10.3.T3745Po 2004 · [E]—dc22 · 2003027538   6 7 8 9 10   05 06 07 08   Printed in Singapore 46   First edition, October 2004
The text type was set in 24-point Neutraface Text Bold. The illustrations are linocuts printed on Thai mulberry bleached rice paper using water-based inks. Book design by Stephen Savage and David Saylor

FOR ROBERT — L. T.   FOR MY PARENTS — S. S.

THE NIGHT IS KEEN AND COLD.

Snug inside her warm den, a polar bear cub wakes.

Something in the moonlit stillness quietly beckons.

What is it?

The little cub leaves her warm,
soft mother, so deep asleep.
She sets out for the snow and sky and
sea and ice, and the moon follows.

Quietly the little cub creeps across the snow,
watching, listening.
All the others are asleep.
She sees the walrus. He is sleeping.

She sees the seals.
They are all sleeping.

She sees the whales.
They are swimming as they sleep.

Farther and farther
the polar bear cub walks,
watching, listening.
Where is she going?
What will she find?

The little bear climbs high
upon a mountain of snow.
There she waits, wondering.
And the moon waits with her.

Then the stars begin to stir.

Over here, stars are softly falling.

Over there, too. It is a star shower.

The stars are like snowflakes, falling, falling.
They light up the snow and the ice.
They light up the lapping waves of the sea.
They light up the walrus and the seals and the whales.

They light up the bear cub's warm, snug den
and her soft, sleeping mother.

They light up everything
the little bear loves.
And the little bear shines bright
with light, too.

One by one, the stars stop falling.
Soon they are still again,
shining upon the little bear,
shining as they sleep.
Now the polar bear cub is ready for sleep, too.

She makes her way back
through the keen, clear night,
and the moon follows.

Snow and sky and sea and ice
and mother bear's soft, warm fur. . . .

HOME.